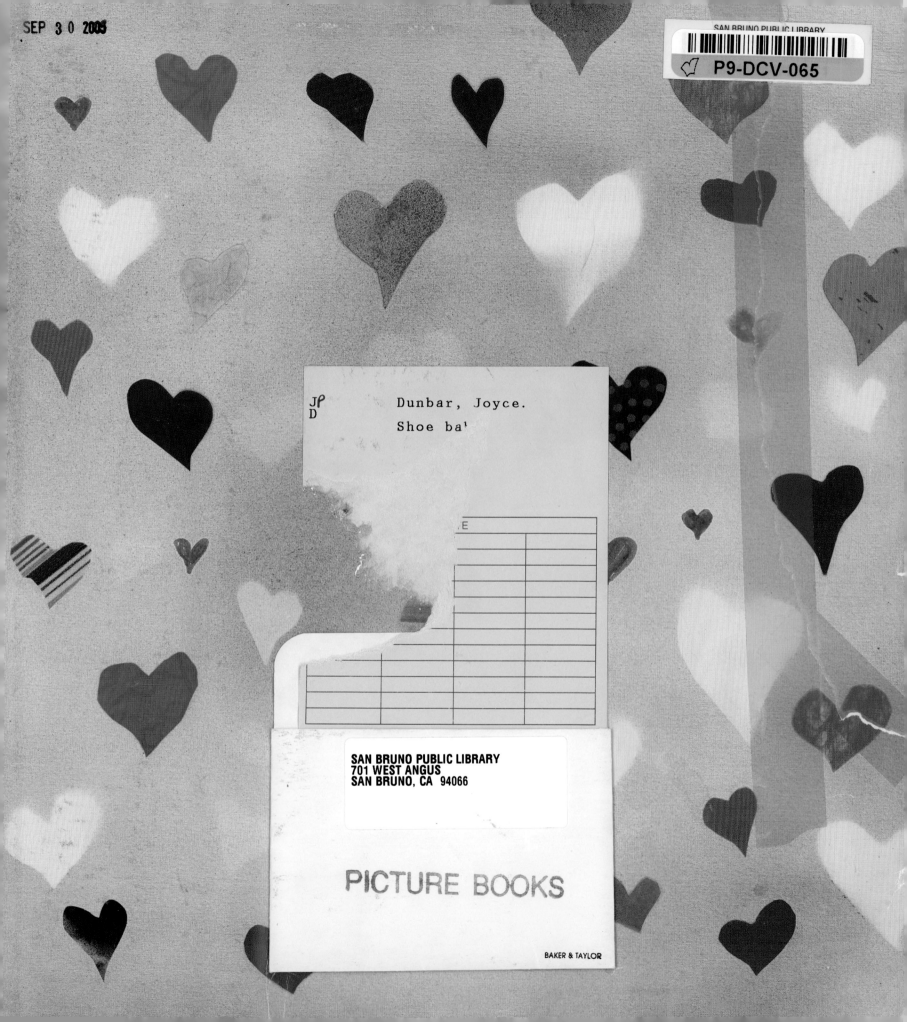

For Jennie Fojtik

Text copyright © 2005 by Joyce Dunbar
Illustrations copyright © 2005 by Polly Dunbar

First U.S. edition 2005

Library of Congress Cataloging-in-Publication Data is available.

Library of Congress Catalog Card Number 2004054614

ISBN 0-7636-2779-8

2 4 6 8 10 9 7 5 3 1

Printed in China

This book was typeset in Godlike Emboldened.
The illustrations were done in mixed media.

Candlewick Press
2067 Massachusetts Avenue
Cambridge, Massachusetts 02140

visit us at www.candlewick.com

CANDLEWICK PRESS
CAMBRIDGE, MASSACHUSETTS

Shoe Baby

Joyce Dunbar

illustrated by

Polly Dunbar

There once was a baby
Who hid in a shoe
And had learned how to say,
"How do you do?"

In a shoe you might think
There is not much to do,
But this very same baby
Went to SEA in that shoe!

A dolphin came by
And an octopus too.
Said this sail-away baby,
"How do you do?"

And this baby I tell you
Went to TOWN in that shoe,
Passing the shops
On the way to the zoo.

At the monkeys he waved
And the elephants too,
And he greeted them all
With a "How do you do?"

This very same baby
FLEW in that shoe!
To the birds of the air he said,
"How do you do?"

Then this fly-away baby
SANG in the shoe.
"Dum-de-dum. Tra-la-la.
How do you do?"

Later, this baby
Had TEA in that shoe!
He invited the Queen
Who brought the King too.

"Good gracious!" they said,
"Pray who are you?"
With a bow said the baby,
"How do you do?"

At long last this baby
Slept in that shoe
So dozy, so cozy,
So tickety-boo.

And he dreamed a bright dream
Of a pink cockatoo,
Saying over and over,
"Toodle-oo! Toodle-oo!"

But now . . . there's a noise . . .
"BOO-HOO-HOO!
BOO-HOO-HOO!"
And a giant comes by
Wearing only one shoe.

And he makes such a fuss

Such a hullabaloo,

Stamping and shouting,

"WHO TOOK
MY SHOE?"

And following fast
Came a giantess too,
Sobbing and sighing,
"BOO-HOO-HOO!
BOO-HOO-HOO!"

And into her polka-dot
Hankie she blew,
"My baby! He's lost!
Oh what shall I do?"

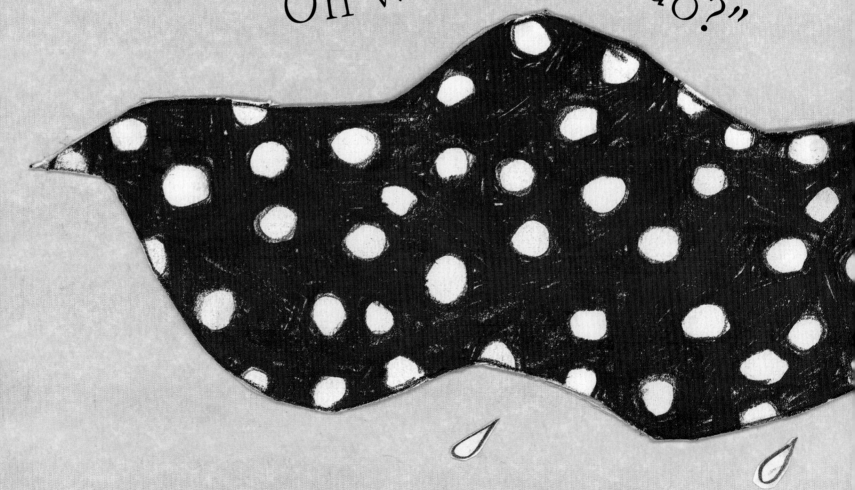

All at once this strange baby

Grew in the shoe.

He grew
and he grew

Right out of that shoe!

"Peekaboo!" said the baby,
Popping up from the shoe.
"Hi, Papa!
Hi, Mama!
How do
you
do?"

"My shoe," said Papa.
"My runaway shoe!
I could find only one,
But now I have two!"

"My baby," said Mama.
"It really is you!
High and low I have looked
but not in a shoe!"

And the baby
just beamed
and said,

"How do you do?"